The Enforcer

BY

Teresa Gabelman

The Enforcer

Gabelman, Teresa (2016-10-31). The Enforcer

Editor: Hot Tree Editing

Chapter 1

Becky Adams elbowed her way through the crowded club trying not to get knocked over or spill her beer. Cursing and fighting her way to a table was not her idea of a good time, and she totally regretted coming. Seeing an opening between the thrashing of dancing bodies, Becky rushed her way through, proud she hadn't spilled a drop of beer. Admittedly, it was the only highlight in her night so far.

"Come on, Bec!" Her best friend, who had talked her into this crazy idea, waved her over.

Finally reaching the tall table with two chairs, Becky grabbed onto it like a lifeline. "Okay, that was nuts." She climbed on the high stool taking a deep breath.

"But totally worth it." Her friend, Sandra Wright, laughed, moving with the music. "It's about damn time you did something other than working and sitting home alone."

Becky raised an eyebrow before taking a long drink of her beer. "I like working and sitting at home alone, thank you very much." Seriously, she had a ton of movies to catch up on and a tub of chocolate ice cream waiting at home for her.

Glancing around while Sandra danced in her seat to the song blaring through the club, Becky sighed. Vamps was the new place in town and the only mixed club in a hundred-mile radius. The club welcomed vampires and humans. It was a little intimidating. Coming from a small town outside of Cincinnati that didn't deal with many vampire visitors didn't help her discomfort, but Sandra could pretty much talk her into anything. That thought made her frown. It was Sandra who introduced her to Maverick Wilder two years earlier. Recently out of a relationship, she hadn't been looking for another, but Maverick wasn't just "another." She'd fallen in love with him, hard and fast. They had been inseparable until the day he disappeared.

"Stop it!" Sandra yelled, pointing at her.

"What?" Sure that she looked guilty, Becky took another drink. Sandra knew her all too well.

"He's gone and the bastard sent you a text." Sandra slammed her drink down. "Screw him. You deserve better than that."

Sandra was right; she did deserve better. He'd been missing for two months before she'd randomly received a text telling her he was sorry, but their relationship just wasn't "doing it for him"—the ass—and "not to try to contact him again." Yeah, that was what she got after a year of what she thought was total bliss. It had broken her heart then, and it broke her heart now. She swore if her heart ever healed, no one would have the power to do to her what Maverick Wilder had done. Every single day she thought of him, and every single day she made that pledge to herself.

"Okay, that's it." Sandra slid off her stool. "I'm going to find you a hot guy."

"Sandra, no!" Becky tried to grab her arm, but Sandra was faster and slipped away.

Looking for the exit sign, she wondered if she could get out before Sandra returned. But no such luck. Sandra headed toward her pulling some poor guy behind her.

"This is Becky," Sandra shouted over the music. "This is... what did you say your name was?"

The man looked nervous; he was sweating and looking around. When Sandra tugged on his arm, he looked down at her then at Becky. "James."

"Well, James." Sandra shoved him at Becky. "Show my friend a good time. She loves to dance."

If Becky could have gotten away with murder, she would have killed Sandra in that instant. But it was still against the law to murder your best friend, so she glared at her in warning before she was led to the dance floor by a very apprehensive James. She had noticed his fangs when he'd said his name, which made her a little nervous, but the security was thick in the club. Seriously, what the hell was he going to do; bite her in a club full of people? Rolling her eyes at herself, she groaned when the DJ picked that minute to play a slow song. Glancing back at a smiling Sandra, she sneered at her before she was pulled into James's arms.

She never remembered being this uncomfortable in her life. Peeking up at him, she noticed he was very handsome but sweated... a lot, and his eyes were all shifty. Okay, all she had to do was get through this dance, kill her friend—she decided the jail time would be worth it—and then go home to her quiet little apartment.

"So, you come here a lot?" Becky figured she might as well make the most of it. "This is actually my first time. It's a pretty nice place." She lied. She hated it, but figured she'd play nice.

The man wasn't even looking at her but over her head. "What?"

"I said, do you come here—" Becky started to repeat what she had said, but the sound of screams over the music cut her short.

"Fuck!" James's grip on her tightened to the point of pain. Trying to pull away, she was unsuccessful; he wouldn't loosen his grip.

"Hey!" Becky clawed at his hands, but her head was turned toward the shouts. Six huge men headed straight toward them dressed in all black; even black bandanas covered the lower part of their faces. Badges, which she couldn't decipher, hung around their necks, but what really caught her attention were the guns aiming straight toward her. Turning, she frantically attempted to pry away from James, but he spun her around, his arm tight around her neck.

"Let the woman go," one of the men ordered, his gun still aimed straight at her since she had become a body shield for the asshole holding her. Even as scared as she was the thought, *Sandra has the worse damn taste in men,* crossed her mind.

"No." James's grip around her neck tightened. "I don't know shit, so just fucking leave me alone. I swear to God, I'll break her fucking neck."

"Whoa!" Becky choked, wiggling and trying to dislodge herself.

"Then you will die." Another man's voice came from behind a bandana, and that voice was somewhat familiar. "So let her go."

"Fuck you!" He started to drag her backward, and that scared her more than anything. There was no way she could leave with this maniac. If she learned anything in her women's self-defense class, it was never to leave crime scene A because you didn't walk away from crime scene B.

With a scream, she reached back and grabbed the man by the balls.

"You bitch!" His high-pitched scream pierced her ears. When he loosened his grip on her neck to grab her hand on his balls, she slammed her head back into his face.

Even though she was loose from the guy, her legs wouldn't work and she fell to her knees. The sound of gunshots rang out, making her cover her ears and head. A loud thud sounded beside her. She peeked to see James staring at her with unseeing eyes and a hole in the middle of his forehead. She couldn't stop staring at the hole; the flesh sizzled around the jagged wound with a thin line of smoke coming out of it.

"Oh, God." Becky finally averted her eyes and started to move away from him, but more shouts stopped her.

4

Who the hell were they yelling at now? She looked up to see all but one of the men pointing their guns at her.

Chapter 2

Becky sat freezing in a small room with nothing but a metal chair that froze her ass. She never wore skirts, but of course, tonight she did. Yeah, her luck sucked and continued to suck. Not only had she gone to a club she didn't want to be at, danced with a vampire she didn't want to dance with, been held hostage by said vampire who threatened to break her neck, and had guns aimed at her, but she was also handcuffed and taken to this shithole of a place where she sat freezing to death. At least they took the handcuffs off. She'd never been handcuffed before and swore to never be handcuffed again.

She'd seen enough television, especially in the past year, to know it was a type of interrogation room. With her ass cheeks numb, she stood and rubbed her arms as she walked toward the large two-way mirror. She knew people were behind it, and it pissed her off. They'd taken her bag and phone, so she had no clue what time it was, but she had been in this room for at least an hour.

"Hey!" She tapped on the glass. "Can I please get a coat or something if this is going to take any longer. I'm literally freezing my ass off on that chair. It's the least you can do since I haven't done a damn THING!" She screamed the last word, then punched the glass. Shit. She grabbed her hand, rubbing it.

She jumped when the door opened. A tall man walked in and slammed it closed behind him. "Have a seat!" he ordered, his dark eyes staring at her as he leaned against the wall, arms crossed.

"I'd rather stand." Becky stuck her chin out in defiance. The man still wore the bandana that covered his nose and mouth. It was quite intimidating, but she would be damned if she let him know that. When the man didn't say a word, but just stared at her, she sighed and sat on the freezing metal chair.

"How do you know James Marshal?" The man's tone was to the point. His relaxed stance and voice contradicted each other.

6

"I don't know him," Becky replied, wondering who in the hell Sandra had grabbed for her to dance with. When he just stared at her, she knew he didn't believe her. "I swear I don't know James Marshal. My friend, *ex*-friend, thought I needed a dancing partner and came back with him."

"Who was he there with?" the man asked, his tone the same.

"Ah, hello." Becky wiggled in the chair, trying to warm it up. Her damn teeth were starting to chatter. Though that could be from nerves, she thought for a second. "I wouldn't know since I don't know who the hell James Marshal is."

When the man just stood there, Becky's anxiety grew.

"Listen, my dad is a retired cop." She lied. Her dad was a truck driver, but he didn't know that. "I've got rights and I want a phone call and my lawyer."

The way the man's eyes crinkled suggested he was smiling.

"I'm not a cop. You have no rights and a lawyer can't help you." The man pushed away from the wall coming within inches from her. "I will ask you one last time. How do you know James Marshal?"

Okay, now she knew for a fact her teeth were not chattering from the cold, but from fear. What the hell had she been dragged into? She had always had smarts, and she knew that this man would eat her alive if she showed an ounce of fear. "And I will tell you one last time. I do not, did not, and never have known James Marshal."

Becky gasped when he grabbed her arm and pulled her up from the chair. It wasn't a painful grip, just abrupt. He opened the door leading her down a long windowless hallway where he opened up another door and shoved her inside before slamming it shut, leaving her alone.

Looking around, Becky wrapped her arms around herself. This room was like the last room, but larger with a long table and two chairs. "At least they aren't metal." She snorted, trying to be a tough guy. She knew she was being watched; she felt it.

******

Maverick Wilder stood behind the two-way mirror and couldn't believe he was staring at Becky fucking Adams. He'd thought he was over her, but seeing her in harm's way at the club told him that was a lie. He was far from over her. What in the fuck was she doing involved with scum like James Marshal?

"She isn't talking." Dale Jackson slammed into the room, glancing at Maverick. "You're up."

"I know her," Maverick said, his eyes still watching Becky. He knew she was scared, though she wouldn't show it. She had always been tough, said whatever came to her mind, and she was strong. Three of the many things he fell in love with.

"What did you say?" Dale frowned when Maverick looked at him.

"I know her," Maverick repeated, then looked back out the two-way.

"How well?" Dale asked, then cursed as if already knowing the answer.

"Very," was Maverick's only reply.

"Oh, shit! That's not good," Dusty Reynolds said from behind the computer he was working on. He then stood, looking out at Becky. "But damn good taste, man. Feisty and hot as hell. Sweet combination. I bet she's a real good fuc—"

Maverick had Dusty by the throat and against the wall before Dale had time to react. "Keep your eyes off her and your fucking mouth shut." Maverick squeezed hard in warning. "You got me?"

"Goddammit, Dusty! You and your fucking mouth." Dale stepped between them. When Maverick released Dusty, Dale pushed him back.

"Okay, damn." Dusty rubbed his throat. "Sorry, Mav. Didn't know you still had a hard-on for the chick."

Maverick started going after Dusty again, but Dale stopped him. "Jasper is out, and he's the only one who can read other than you. Can you do this?"

With one last glare at Dusty, Maverick nodded. This was his fucking job, and he was damn good at it. Plus, he didn't have a choice. They needed to move fast on this so it was up to him. "Yeah, no problem."

"Just keep your fucking mask up and I'll ask the questions." Dale rubbed his eyes and sighed. "Is her dad really a cop?"

"No, he's a truck driver." Maverick actually grinned, grabbed his bandana, and headed toward the door. He wasn't surprised when Becky had lied. She had a quick wit.

"You sure you can handle this?" Dale looked from the mirror back to Maverick.

Maverick really didn't know the answer to that question, so he remained silent. He walked out the door, slamming it behind him. Once in the hallway, he leaned against the door, closed his eyes and cursed. He needed to end this fast and get her the fuck out of there for both their sakes.

Chapter 3

Becky picked up one of the two chairs and headed toward the mirror. She was pissed, scared, and she had to pee… really bad. Beer always made her have to pee, as well as nerves, so yeah, she was damn uncomfortable. She had asked repeatedly to use the restroom knowing they could hear her because she saw the microphone, but no one would answer her. Since they ignored her request, she was about to get their attention real quick with this chair.

The door slammed open making her scream; the chair over her head aimed toward the two-way mirror. She immediately noticed this was not the same man from before. He was much bigger and wore a baseball hat pulled so low that between the hat and bandana, she could barely see his eyes. He took two large steps toward her, grabbed the chair and slammed it down, then pointed at it.

"No," she answered his unspoken request for her to sit. "I have been asking to use the restroom and until I do, I will not cooperate."

The man actually snorted but glanced at the mirror. Within seconds, another man walked into the room.

"Come on." He motioned for her to come, but his eyes fell on the other man. "Don't worry. I won't touch."

Becky walked toward the man who had just opened the door. How many bandana-masked men were there? Giving him a strange look, she then cast her eyes back to the other man who had sat in one of the chairs. His black eyes stared at her. She turned her gaze to the man at the door.

"You're damn right you won't," Becky replied with a huff, even though he wasn't talking to her.

"You sure do have a mouth on you." The man shook his head. "I would think you'd be shaking in that little skirt."

The man behind them slammed his hand on the table.

"It takes more than a stupid-looking bandana to scare me." Becky figured she was in shock from watching a man die, being handcuffed, and taken somewhere by strange men because she was saying some really dumb shit.

"Come on, before you get me killed." The man nudged her out of the room and down the hall. Stopping at another door, he shoved it open. "Don't lock it."

Becky closed the door in his face and turned to the toilet in the small bathroom. Obviously no women were around because this bathroom was disgusting and smelled of old piss. Lifting her skirt, she started to sit, but stopped and glanced at the door. Turning on the water, she hovered over the nasty toilet and peed and peed, and then freaking peed some more. Finally finishing, she looked around for toilet paper and typically, her luck still sucked. She thought about calling out, but figured it would be useless. Reaching over, she grabbed the paper towels, cleaned herself up then flushed the paper towel down the toilet, hoping it stopped it up. Yeah, she was in bitch mode. Washing her hands, she took her time looking around for any means of escape, but there wasn't any. It was a tiny room with no windows, just a sink, toilet, and no toilet paper. Wanting to irritate the asshole on the other side of the door, she waited a few more minutes before opening the door.

"That was disgusting." Becky grimaced as she headed back to the room where the other man stood just outside the door watching them. He then disappeared inside.

"Sorry it wasn't up to your standards, your majesty." The man nudged her in and slammed the door behind her.

Once again, alone with the man who hadn't said a word to her,

Becky's insides started to shake. Her stomach pitched violently with nerves. He pushed the empty chair with his booted foot with a nod.

"I don't know what else I can say to you people." Becky frowned when her voice cracked. She sat in the chair because honestly, she didn't know how long her legs were going to hold her. Her brave façade was quickly cracking.

"What is your involvement with James Marshal?" A voice echoed through the room, and it didn't come from the man sitting directly in front of her.

The man staring intently at her grabbed her wrist in a tight grip.

"Hey, get off me." She tried to pull away, but he held on tight. "I've told you, my friend pulled the man over for me to dance with. It's as simple as that. I do not know that man and nothing you do to me will change that fact."

The man let go of her quickly, looking up at the mirror with a nod as he stood. Becky wrapped her arms around herself, not knowing what had just happened or what to expect next. He went to move, but stopped, taking off the black leather jacket he wore and tossing it onto the table. That was when her eye caught something very familiar.

Without thinking of what she was doing, she grabbed his tattooed arm turning it before he could pull away. She gasped, seeing her name tattooed over a thick bold infinity symbol. Only one man she knew had that tattoo.

"Maverick?" she whispered, confused as her eyes shot from the tattoo to the man who remained rigid until he pulled his arm away and walked out of the room.

******

Taking his hat and bandana off, Maverick passed all the rooms heading straight outside, his steps quick. Bursting through the door, bright sunlight blinded him, but he didn't care. He needed to get the fuck out of there.

"Fuck!" he cursed, slamming his fist against the concrete building. Welcoming the pain, he did it again.

The door opened behind him, but he didn't turn around. Instead, he closed his eyes trying to calm his emotions.

"I had Dusty take her to a holding cell," Dale informed him. "We need to decide what to do with her now that she knows who you are. I'll call in a scrubber."

"And if that doesn't work?" Maverick tried to keep the growl out of his voice.

"Then we'll figure something else out," Dale replied after a minute of hesitancy.

Maverick turned, his eyes narrowed on his boss. "She will not be harmed in any way." It was not a question, but a fact that he vowed to see through.

"She will not be harmed." Dale nodded in agreement. "We are not in the business of harming innocents, Maverick, and you know that. I think your feelings for this woman are clouding your judgment."

Maverick watched him go back inside. His feelings for Becky had always clouded his judgment, but not in a bad way as far as he was concerned. Leaning against the wall, he looked down at the tattoo on his arm, remembering the day he got it. He remembered every single second of that day.

But things had changed, he had changed, his world had changed, and he would not bring her into his dangerous world. He'd fought himself every single fucking day not to bring her into the hell he lived daily and yet, there she was, more beautiful than he ever remembered, right smack in the middle of it.

With another curse, he pushed away from the wall and went back inside. Walking into the watch room, he glanced at the interrogation room, his jacket laying where he had tossed it. Grabbing his phone and wallet, he headed out then stopped.

"Make sure she has a blanket, food, and water," he told Dusty and didn't wait for a response. He knew Dusty would make sure his orders were followed; he just didn't want to hear Dusty's mouth. He wasn't in the mood.

Chapter 4

Becky lay on the hard bench numb to everything and not because she was in a jail cell. Instead, her reaction was focused on being face-to-face, so to speak, with a man she never thought she'd see again. Despite her secret hopes she would see that man again, now that she had, her heart hurt more than ever.

A tear escaped and she wiped it away angrily, tugging the blanket under her chin. The man who had taken her to the bathroom earlier had brought her a blanket and food; the latter still sat by the door. Her stomach rumbled, but she refused to eat anything. He had come in a couple of times to see if she needed to use the restroom and told her she needed to eat, but Becky ignored him. Screw them. She wanted to go home. She'd answered their stupid questions.

They even had some guy come in, grab her by the head with both hands, and place his thumbs on her temples. When she'd started fighting him, two others came in to hold her down. Obviously, whatever they were trying to do didn't work because the guy walked out pissed off. Good, 'cause she was pissed off too.

She knew Sandra had to be freaking out. She had been locked up for at least twelve hours or possibly more at a guess. The door opened, light spilling into her face. Squinting, she looked up without moving her head, and there he stood with no bandana or hat hiding his face.

"You need to eat something." He glanced down at the untouched food. Immediately, she knew why he hadn't spoken earlier. There was no mistaking his deep raspy rumble.

"I want to go home." She stayed exactly where she was. Hunger made her stomach ache, but his betrayal cemented her stubbornness.

"Dammit, Becky!" He huffed, walking closer to her. "What in the hell were you doing at Vamps dancing with that scumbag?"

As pissed as she was by his outburst, she couldn't help but notice how damn handsome he still was. His raven black hair was longer than she had ever seen it, his face more masculine, but his fangs were brand new. "How long have you been a vampire?"

"I'm asking the questions, dammit."

"Well, I have questions of my own." She sneered, sitting up. "Like what in the hell was that guy trying to do to me with his hands on my head? Or what in the hell have you gotten yourself into? Better yet, what in the hell have I gotten myself into? Or how about why after two months of being missing, did you send me a text saying get lost? Hmmm, how about you answer those and then I'll answer yours."

"There are only certain things I'm at liberty to discuss with you." Maverick stared down at her. "And we tried to scrub your memory."

"Excuse me?" Becky stood. "You tried to do what to my memory?"

"Calm down, Becky." Maverick sighed. "It didn't work."

Becky took a step and slapped him across the face. "How's that for calm, asshole." That anger was too much for her to take. Once one tear fell, the floodgates opened. "Damn you, Maverick."

******

Never in his life had he ever felt this helpless. The brave, smart-ass Becky he could handle, but the broken, crying Becky was damn near killing him. "Becky, listen to me." He reached out, but she smacked his hands away, so he dropped them. "I never wanted to hurt you and believe it or not, I'm trying to keep you safe."

Swiping angrily at her tears, Becky stared up at him. "I don't understand any of this." She flipped her arms out.

"I know you don't, hon—" Maverick stopped himself, wondering what in the hell he was doing.

"Don't you dare call me that." Becky glared at him, her eyes red from the tears. "Don't you even dare."

Maverick decided then and there, no matter the consequences to him, she deserved the truth. "Sit down," he ordered, noticing her swaying.

"Don't tell me what to do." She frowned up at him.

"Still like to argue, I see." Maverick actually grinned. "Sit down and I'll answer your questions."

Surprise mixed with doubt flitted across her face, but she sat on the bench and wrapped her arms around herself with a shiver.

"You're also still hardheaded as hell." Maverick reached for the blanket and the water. Wrapping the blanket around her, he handed her the bottle, which she took.

"I haven't changed." Becky shrugged. "I'm still the same person I was a year ago."

Maverick had to disagree. She was more beautiful, but he kept that to himself. Her red hair, highlighted by the summer sun, still looked soft and framed her heart-shaped face. Her eyes were still as sea green as he remembered, but the sadness he saw reflected in their depths stabbed at him.

"The night I was supposed to pick you up at work I was attacked." Maverick felt telling her what happened was a much safer topic. The more he looked at her, the more he wanted to take her in his arms. He missed her touch, missed being inside her, missed everything about her. He craved her and it had only grown worse over time. There had been no other women and he seriously doubted there ever would be. "I don't remember it. The only thing I remember is waking up with fangs and a thirst for blood."

With wide eyes, Becky stared at him, wrapping the cover around her tightly. She didn't say a word as she listened.

"The first man who talked to you found me and brought me here." Maverick crossed his arms and leaned against the bars of the cell. "I was so angry after I found out what happened to me that I joined with him and the others. We are known in the vampire world as Enforcers. We protect innocents and humans. The man you were dancing with is someone we've been hunting for a long time. He's responsible for over a hundred human women being turned into vampires. Once they're turned, they are sold as high-dollar whores, slaves, or whatever the buyer wants them for. We hide our identity because many times we go undercover in order to buy women."

"So it was that easy to walk away from me?" Becky tilted her head, her question asked point-blank.

"Yes, because I had nothing to offer you," Maverick replied without hesitation, yet he knew that was a lie. It killed him to walk away from her, but it was better that she believed otherwise. There was no future for them.

Chapter 5

Becky's mind spun. Maverick was a vampire. He totally walked away from her and what they shared because he had nothing to offer her. He was an Enforcer—not that she knew what that was—and he protected innocents and humans. And she was nothing to him. It cut like a knife. It hurt worse than his unfeeling text, and all she wanted to do was fall into his arms and beg him to hold her, but she'd slit her own throat before admitting to any of that.

"When can I go home?" She removed the blanket, tossing it to the ground. "There are people who are worried about me, and I have a job."

"The reason we had to try to scrub you is for your safety. The less you know, the safer you are." Maverick ignored her question and statement.

"Honestly, Maverick, I'm going to forget this whole situation as soon as I leave this fucking building, so no worries there." Becky ran her hand through her hair, trying her best to act like someone who didn't give a shit, but what a lie that was.

She wanted so badly to see some kind of emotion from him, but he talked to her as a stranger, not like a man who had known her every secret, her every fear, and her every dream. A man who had touched every inch of her body with those large hands, and who she had given her virginity to. No, this man was a stranger with only a familiar face. She knew for a fact her heart would never mend. This break could never be sealed.

Before either one of them could say anything else, the door opened and this time, the man who she'd first met walked in without his bandana. "Ms. Adams, thank you for your cooperation," he said, glancing at Maverick then back at her. "I'm sorry for your inconvenience, but until we knew for sure that you had no connections to James Marshal, we couldn't let you go."

Becky wanted to snort at that but held it back. She was too numb to even be sarcastic at that moment. "Am I free to go?" was all she said.

"Yes, we have someone ready to take you home." He frowned. "But to protect our agents, I'd like to ask that you refrain from talking to anyone about this."

A sad smile slid across her face, her eyes landing on Maverick. "It's already forgotten."

The man cleared his throat but nodded. "Thank you."

Becky didn't say anything else. She grabbed her bag and phone he handed her then followed him out the door without looking at Maverick. However, she felt his eyes on her and wished she felt nothing, but she felt too much. Biting her lip hard, she tasted blood.

She followed the man down the hallway and out into the night, knowing she had left the rest of her heart in a cold jail cell with a man who didn't care.

******

Maverick stood in the cell watching her go, the emptiness overwhelming him. Once she was out of sight, he continued to stand there, his mind and heart at war with each other. Being turned into a vampire had in no way changed his feelings for Becky. Nothing short of death could do that. She was the love of his life; he knew that, accepted that, yet his choices after being changed had taken him far away from her.

He had been so bitter that his life had been altered by no fault of his own that if it wasn't for Dale and the rest of the Enforcers, he would probably be one they hunted down. He had taken an oath to serve and protect. What they did was dangerous and few Enforcers had relationships.

He refused to put Becky through the hell, and even though he had to fight to stay planted inside the cell instead of running after her, he knew it was for the best. When he'd seen her dancing with that bastard, he'd wanted to kill him for just having his hands on Becky, and that was exactly the reason he'd never sought her out. She was a beautiful woman, and any man would be lucky to have her, but he knew himself well. If he found her with another man, he would more than likely kill the son of a bitch.

"You okay, man?" Dusty stuck his head inside the door.

Maverick didn't reply, just gave a short nod.

"Listen, I'm sorry. I shouldn't have disrespected your lady like that." Dusty's apology was sincere.

"She's not my lady." Maverick growled, yet he knew she would always be just that in his mind.

"Yeah, well... bullshit." Dusty walked the rest of the way in. "I always knew something was off with you, and now I know what it is. Her. So why are you letting her walk away? You've gotten your revenge on the bastards who turned you. You have a job making a shit ton of money, and you're crazy about her."

"What the hell is this?" Maverick turned to glare at Dusty. "It's Your Life, Oprah Edition?"

"I knew you had a sense of humor." Dusty snorted. "But no, I'm a hell of a lot smarter than Oprah. This is a 'get your head out of your ass' speech."

"Dusty, I appreciate... whatever the hell you're trying to accomplish, but back the fuck off." Maverick started past him before he killed him.

"I don't think we've seen the last of your woman... just sayin'," Dusty called out before Maverick could completely walk out of the

21

cell.

Maverick stopped with a frown. "What?"

"Well, I know you've been preoccupied with your head up your ass—"

"You have no clue how close you are to having your head shoved up your own ass," Maverick warned, taking a step toward a smirking Dusty.

"Hey, I'm just saying, depending on who else was at the club, it's very likely we weren't the only ones who saw her dancing with James." Dusty turned serious, all joking aside. "If that's the case, others may think she has a connection. James owed a lot of people money and with him dead, they may go after anyone connected to him."

Maverick cursed. Dusty was right; his head had been up his ass because he knew this, but failed to see it. "Hit our connections hard to find out who, if any, of our scum on the lists were in that club," Maverick ordered, his mind already racing and his protective instincts kicking into high gear.

"Already on it, big guy. I also have her address, place of employment and well, pretty much her entire life. Awesome what you can find with good old Google. Unless you already have that information." Dusty held up a small memory stick.

Grabbing the memory stick, Maverick frowned. He didn't have anything on her because he knew if he had searched her out, he wouldn't have been able to walk away again. He had stayed away knowing she was better off without him.

Chapter 6

"Are you sure nothing happened to you?" Sandra watched Becky bring back another plate of food. "You never get orders wrong."

"He didn't say cheese," Becky replied, putting the plate back up. Even Earl, the cook, shot her a strange look.

"Come on, Becky." Sandra grabbed a plate Earl put in the window, setting it on her tray. "You haven't been acting right since last night. I've been a mess since then, and I wasn't taken away by undercover agents."

Becky's agitation grew. She hated keeping anything from her best friend, but talking about it made it more real. That was the last thing she wanted because if it was real, it meant Maverick would never walk back into her life and sweep her away. Yeah, that had been her secret dream for a year and it was sad, so very sad.

"The food is getting cold." Becky nodded, still waiting for the cheese to get slapped on the hamburger she'd brought back.

"Ugh!" Sandra took off with a hiss.

Becky straightened the counter then turned to look around. The dinner crowd had come and gone, only a few regulars remained. She loved working at the Country Inn Restaurant. She earned enough money for her small apartment, few bills, and food while her tips went into savings to someday buy the restaurant from Marcy Reynolds.

There weren't many places of work to choose from in her small town of Alexandria, Kentucky. She had worked here part-time in high school, decided against college and continued at the restaurant where she was happy. She loved to cook and did all the cooking on the days Earl was off. Marcy had taught her everything she knew about the business and was just waiting on Becky so she could retire and sell to her. Becky hoped in the next year she would have enough for a nice down payment on a loan.

"Order up, Becky," Earl called out behind her, breaking into her thoughts.

Grabbing the plate, she headed for the table, setting it down in front of the customer with an apology. She glanced out of the window which ran the whole front of the restaurant. The black Mustang GT she had admired earlier in the day during the lunch rush still sat there. The windows were tinted and with night approaching, she couldn't tell if someone was in there or not. Only two customers remained, and she knew they didn't drive the Mustang. With a frown, she turned back to the counter.

"Do you know who owns the Mustang?" Becky asked Sandra and then Earl.

"No, but I wish I did." Sandra grinned, glancing that way. "That car is the shit."

Nodding, Becky got busy cleaning the dinner mess and once again forgot about the car that sat alone in the parking lot.

"Hey, I gotta go. My stuff is done," Sandra said, heading toward the back parking lot. "I'll see ya tomorrow."

"Sounds good." Becky waved, wiping down one of the tables. "Be careful."

"You need help out there, Becky?" Earl asked from the kitchen.

"Nope, I'm good." She smiled with a nod. "Have a good night, Earl. See you tomorrow."

Becky started on the last table and was glad the day was done. She'd had a total of two hours sleep in the last twenty-four hours;

she was dead tired.

"Kitchen's closed," she called out when the door opened. Looking up, she knocked the salt shaker off the table, and it rolled across the floor, stopping at the tip of Maverick Wilder's boots.

She watched in surprise as he bent over and picked it up, then walked toward her, setting it back on the table.

"What are you doing here?" Becky finally found her voice. The last time she had seen him here, he had given her a sweet kiss, promised to pick her up after her shift, but never showed. The memory hurt.

"We need to talk." Maverick stared down at her. "Now."

******

Maverick had sat in his car watching every move Becky made. He couldn't believe she still worked at the restaurant. The whole time he sat outside, he observed the men she served watching her walk away. They focused on her longer than Maverick was comfortable with. Too many times to count he had to talk himself down before he walked in there and tossed every fucker with a dick out the window.

Finally, the place had cleared and Sandra had driven away. He knew the other car wasn't Becky's since she lived right across the street in the small apartment complex, so he had waited for that car to leave also. He had parked away from the restaurant to do a run-through and had seen the cars in the back. He had also checked out her apartment from the outside and wasn't happy about that setup for safety. After he had finished his recon, he had gone back to his car and drove to the restaurant, parking in front to keep an eye on Becky.

When Becky didn't reply to his request, he walked over to a booth in the back, away from the window, facing the door and sat down.

25

He cocked his eyebrow at her when she just stood and stared.

Finally with a sigh, she slapped the rag she was using to clean tables with on the counter, grabbed two cups and poured coffee. He watched as she fixed hers with tons of sugar and cream, then added one spoonful of sugar and no cream to his. He was pleased she remembered how he took his coffee.

"What wasn't said last night that you had to come all the way out here to tell me?" Becky set the coffee on the table before sitting down across from him.

He watched as she rolled her neck, then reached up and massaged it, closing her eyes for a second.

"I can't believe you still work here." And he couldn't believe he just fucking said that. This was to be straight business and he was really fucking that up by wanting to throw men out windows, being pleased that she remembered his coffee, and now wanting to massage her neck with his mouth.

"Yeah, well, not many places to work around this small town and I have all I need." Becky eyed him. "What do you want, Maverick?"

And wasn't that a loaded question? "You may be in danger." He frowned, taking a long drink of his coffee. She still made it with a kick, just the way he liked it.

"From who?" Becky's eyes widened in confusion. "And why?"

"We don't know exactly who was at the club last night, and there are a lot of people who have been looking for James. We think he was trying to make a connection, but things got out of control before we could find out for sure." Maverick watched her reaction, which appeared thoughtful and cool. "There's talk that people have been asking about you."

"People?" Becky frowned, her hands fidgeting. It was something he remembered her always doing when she was nervous. "What people?"

"People you don't want asking about you," Maverick responded. "This is serious, Becky. Until we know for sure, you need to have around-the-clock protection."

"This is absurd." Becky shook her head. "I have nothing to do with that man. What in the hell would people be asking about me for? I don't understand any of this."

Maverick sighed, knowing this was exactly why he had cut ties with her. Even thinking she was in danger was driving him fucking insane.

"He owed people money, people you don't want to owe anything to. Seeing you dancing with him is where the connection is coming from." Maverick didn't want to scare her, but he wanted her to know how serious this was.

"But—"

"It doesn't matter, Becky." Maverick shook his head then finished off his coffee. "The connection was made."

Maverick let her soak that in for a few minutes before breaking the news that her life was about to be turned upside down.

"So what am I going to do?" Becky actually glanced out the window, her eyes searching as if someone was going to pop out of the shadows.

"I'm not going to let anyone hurt you," Maverick promised, his voice deep and hard. "But you are going to have to cooperate and listen to me."

The narrowed eyes and frown clued him in that this may be a fight.

"To you?" Becky bit her bottom lip, another nervous habit he remembered. "Why you?"

Because he didn't trust anyone else to keep her safe, but he kept that to himself. "Because we have a past, and it will be easier to explain why I'm with you twenty-four seven." Maverick waited for the slap, but it didn't come... yet. "The story would be I was attacked, changed, had amnesia, regained my memory and came back to you."

Becky stared at him wide-eyed. "That is seriously what you came up with?" She snorted. "Sounds like a bad Lifetime movie. No way will that work."

"It will work." Maverick gave her a nod. "Just follow my lead."

"It's not going to work. And how are you going to explain the sweet text you sent me?" Becky frowned without meeting his eyes. That text still stung. "Sandra will see through it."

"Sandra isn't who I'm worried about, but I will handle Sandra." Maverick stood, reached over and pulled her to him. "And it starts now."

Chapter 7

Becky wanted this—no, she didn't—but really she did. "No." She came to her senses pushing against him, but he didn't budge. "Maverick, stop."

He held her still, clipping her chin with his hand, lifting her face to his. "This needs to be as real as possible, Becky."

It was too real for her; that was the damn problem. "I can't do this." She glared up at him. "I really can't. I'll take my chances."

"You have no idea what you're talking about because you have no clue who may be coming for you." Maverick moved away. "Trust me, as soon as we know you are safe, I'm gone."

Those words hit Becky like a brick to the chest, finally and clearly penetrating her dazed brain. He was gone, kept repeating in her mind. She wasn't a stupid person. Obviously, he would know if she were in danger and yeah, she was afraid. So she would have to bite the bullet, let him do whatever he did to keep her safe, but guard herself. It wasn't a matter of falling in love with him because she'd never stopped. Instead, it was a matter of losing herself again when he disappeared, and she knew that was exactly what was going to happen. He'd said as much.

"Are you done here?" His voice brought her out of her soul-searching moment.

She nodded as she walked away to the kitchen to check that everything was off and locked. Heading back to the front, she grabbed her bag and keys. Maverick opened the door, stepping out first. She noticed him searching the area before letting her out the door. She turned and locked it, then took off across the parking lot, but he grabbed her arm leading her to the passenger side of his car.

"But my apartment is just over there." Becky pointed before being nudged into the seat. The door closed quickly behind her, and then he was sitting in the driver seat, revving the engine. He backed out, put it in Drive and drove across the street and parked. "Okay, well that was strange, but whatever." When she went to get out of the car, he stopped her.

"Wait until I open the door," he ordered, then slid out of the car, walked around the front and opened her door. She slowly pulled herself out and was surprised when he wrapped his arm around her and led her to her apartment. She lifted her key to unlock the door, but he took it from her, unlocked it and cautiously went inside.

She hated to admit it, but it was pretty fascinating watching him work, and she knew that was exactly what he was doing. He pulled her inside shutting the door, his eyes searching her apartment in one sweep. "Wait here."

Becky did as he told her, her eyes wide and heart pumping. She didn't know if her racing heart was because she was afraid someone was in her apartment or because Maverick Wilder was in her apartment. He walked around, checking her bathroom and then her bedroom. When he walked out of the room, she tossed her purse on the counter.

"All clear?" She cocked her eyebrow. Even though she thought he was damn impressive, she wasn't about to let him know that.

"You have one entrance?" He frowned down at her. When she nodded, he cursed. "A death trap."

"Oh, well great." Becky kicked off her shoes. "I'll sleep so much better with those comforting words."

"One entrance and ground floors are the worse safety measures, especially for a woman living alone." Maverick filled her small apartment to the point she felt claustrophobic.

"Yeah, not much to pick from in this town and I like it," she replied, heading toward her bedroom. After grabbing some sweats and a T-shirt, she headed toward the bathroom. "There's soda and beer in the fridge," she offered before disappearing inside the bathroom. Even as upset as she was with him, she couldn't help being a decent hostess, and it pissed her off. She was mad as hell, and yet still worried about his stupid comfort.

Slamming the door, she leaned against it, holding her clothes close to her chest. Leaning her head back with eyes squeezed shut, Becky prayed. She may be safe from whoever may be looking for her, but she definitely wasn't safe from Maverick Wilder.

******

Maverick heard the shower and groaned. Jesus, this was going to be harder than he thought. Her smell was unique and with his more powerful senses, her special scent surrounded him. He breathed in deeply, then cursed. Heading to the fridge, he grabbed a beer wishing it were a shot of whiskey. Walking to one of the only two windows in the small apartment, he glanced out to see if anything seemed out of place, but all looked clear.

The shower continued, and so did his memories. He knew every single beautiful crease, bump, and curve of her sweet body. The way the water ran down her luscious body was burned in his memory. "Fuck. Fuck. Fuck!" he cursed, but it didn't help. The beer didn't help, nothing short of… hell, he couldn't even think of anything that would take his memories of her away.

He finally forced himself and his hard-on under control by the time she came out of the bathroom. Her hair was wet; she liked to let it dry naturally. Turning his head toward the window again, he rolled his eyes at himself. Damn, he was fucking pathetic.

"I have some leftover lasagna," she said, making him turn toward her. His eyes went directly to her ass that was pointed straight at him in those tight sweatpants as she reached in the refrigerator. "You want some?"

31

Maverick groaned, swallowing hard. Not having sex for a year, and having the woman he craved more than anything bent over asking if he wanted *some* was almost too much for his self-control. Finally she stood. Turning, she put the pan of lasagna on the counter. He took a drink of beer as his eyes went straight to her nipples that reached toward him as if begging for his touch and began choking and sputtering beer everywhere. Son of a bitch, she was going to kill him.

"Ah, you okay?" Becky stared at him while plating some lasagna.

His phone rang at that moment. *Thank God.* He nodded as he walked away, clearing his throat before he answered the phone. "Yeah." He cleared his throat again.

"You okay, man?" Dusty asked after a second.

"Yeah, good," Maverick said finally with a normal voice. His eyes caught Becky pointing to the lasagna. Shaking his head, he watched as she turned, bent over and put it away. She was definitely wearing a thong or nothing at all. He groaned again.

"Dude, what the fuck is going on?" Dusty's voice in his ear almost made him drop the phone he forgot he was holding. "You need back up?"

"What the fuck do you want?" Maverick growled, gaining a wide-eyed look from Becky, who turned to the microwave.

"Sexy Becky is getting to ya, isn't she?" Dusty chuckled on the other end of the phone and then made wolf calls.

"I swear if you don't tell me something productive in the next second, I will hunt you down and tear your throat out," Maverick threatened, and anyone who knew Maverick didn't take his threats lightly.

"Okay, chill out." Dusty chuckled. "We got a hit on a Devin

DeMarco. He's real curious about Becky. Seems old worm-food James owed him the most, over five hundred thousand. Yeah, you heard me right. Big chunk of moolah. I just emailed you a pic of him and his thugs."

"Anything else?" Maverick's anger heightened, knowing now that Becky was at risk.

"Yeah, give Becky a smooch for me and—"

Maverick hung up on him. With a shake of his head, he checked his e-mail on his phone. Hitting the attached pictures, they uploaded. He memorized the face of the man who was most likely going to die by his hand because no one was going to harm one hair on Becky's head. Not while he was alive.

******

Becky sat on the couch, with her plate of lasagna watching *The Bachelorette*. Okay, she was sitting on the couch picking at her food staring blindly at the television. Every fiber of her being was focused on the man, who she never thought she'd ever see again, sitting on the other side of her small couch.

"Are you sure you're not hungry?" Becky asked, stabbing at her food.

"I'm good, but thanks." Maverick's deep voice filled her tiny apartment, everything about him filled her tiny apartment. A thought occurred to her. "Do you even eat food?" She slid a glance toward him.

"I do. I only need blood occasionally now that I'm a mature vampire," he replied, then his eyes narrowed. "What in the hell is this?"

Becky glanced at the television, seeing the bachelorette kissing one of the guys. "It's *The Bachelorette*."

"Since I've sat down, I've seen her kiss five different guys." Maverick frowned.

"Well, all those guys are trying to win her over, and she's trying to find love." Becky grinned, figuring television wasn't a big part of his life. Though, she shouldn't be surprised. Maverick had never really been a big television person.

"How in the hell can you find love when you have five different tongues down your throat?" Maverick glared at her. "You seriously watch this shit?"

"Yeah, and I think she should pick Luke." Becky pointed at the handsome cowboy, who was now about ready to kiss her. "He's—"

"A fucking pussy for letting four other guys kiss her." Maverick shook his head in disgust. "If that was the woman I wanted, no man would be putting his hands on her."

His words hit her hard. She used to be that woman, but not anymore. The knowledge was more than she could take. Standing, she took her plate across the room to her kitchen, dropped it in the sink without even scraping the uneaten food off and headed to her bedroom, shutting the door. Knowing she couldn't be that rude, she sighed, wishing she were more of a bitch. Grabbing a pillow off her bed and a blanket out of her closet, she opened her door and walked out. Without saying a word or looking at Maverick, she put the pillow and blanket next to him. Turning, she went back to her bedroom, closing the door behind her.

Switching off her light, she crawled into bed, put her face in the pillow and let the tears flow. Him talking about what he would or would not allow with the woman he loved tore at her. No, that wasn't even close to what she was feeling. Her whole body hurt, not just her heart. Her throat felt tight with a scream of pain that she fought to keep quiet. Her mind raced with what ifs and she couldn't stop it. She was stuck in a nightmare that just kept playing over and over. How could she hate someone she loved more than anything in the world? She would survive this, again. She unfortunately had no choice.

Chapter 8

"Oh, my God!" Sandra hugged Maverick then Becky, and clapped her hands with an excited scream before she hugged Maverick again. "I can't believe this. And you're a vampire." She reached up toward his mouth, but Maverick caught her hand with a chuckle.

"Calm down, Sandra." Becky rolled her sleep-deprived eyes.

"I knew something like this had to have happened." Sandra squealed. "You two were too much in love for you to just up and leave her."

"That's right." Maverick pulled Becky close, giving her a hug, his eyes telling her that he had been right. Sandra believed every word and hadn't even questioned the text.

Becky plastered a fake smile on her face, pinching Maverick's stomach before pushing away. "Come on, we have hungry people who are going to be showing up. We have a lot to do."

"Okay. Okay." Sandra grinned, practically skipping to the back of the restaurant. "Don't leave!" she yelled back at Maverick.

Once she was in the back, Maverick chuckled. "Told you she'd believe it."

Becky smacked him on the arm. "Don't look so smug."

Maverick smirked, heading to the back booth where he could see everything in the restaurant, plus the parking lot as well as a clear shot to the door. Sitting down, he watched Becky go about her routine; it was as if he'd never left. How many damn times had he sat while she prepped for the morning rush? He was surprised when she brought him coffee.

He frowned though when he noticed the pinched look on her face.

He knew she hadn't slept last night. He had heard her crying, his hearing superb. It took everything he had to stay planted on the couch and not go into her bedroom and pull her into his arms. But he'd known that would lead to other things that would only make it harder on them both when he left.

During the morning breakfast crowd, he was alert to everyone who entered. Admittedly, he was more alert of the men who checked out Becky's ass as she walked away or her breasts when she bent over to refill their coffee.

His attention snapped to Becky, who headed his way with a plate of food. "I know you have to be hungry." She set the plate of two eggs over easy, sausage and toast in front of him. "Eat," she ordered and then she was off again.

It wasn't until after the lunch rush that Becky made her way back over to him. Sandra had picked up his dirty dishes and refilled his coffee.

"You have to be bored, Maverick." Becky stared down at him. "I'm sure I'll be fine if you want to take off for a while."

"Not happening." Maverick leaned back to look up at her.

She shrugged. "Suit yourself." She turned to walk away, but stopped and sighed. "Do you need anything?"

"No, I'm fine." He grinned at her back. He knew she was trying her best to be a bitch, but she could never pull it off. Becky was a people person and was always trying to take care of someone.

With the customers slowing down, Maverick glanced at his phone to check his e-mail and messages. He knew he had a lot from all the buzzing his phone was doing, but he had been too vigilant watching for problems.

He finished answering the messages, which weren't many, and

decided to wait for the e-mails. Setting his phone down, he settled back. Sandra was running around cleaning and checking on customers. After a few minutes of not seeing Becky, he leaned forward looking toward the kitchen but didn't see her. He knew she wasn't in the restroom because she would have had to pass him. Feeling a spark of unease, he stood.

"Sandra, where's Becky?" he asked loudly, his eyes still searching as he started walking toward the middle of the restaurant.

"She's taking the garbage to the dumpster," Sandra called out, her hands full of dirty dishes.

"Goddammit!" Maverick leaped over tables void of customers as he ran toward the back through the kitchen.

******

Becky scraped plates into a full garbage can. Setting the plates down, she started to pull the bag out.

"I'll get that as soon as I finish this order," Earl called out over his shoulder.

Becky glanced over at Earl seeing all the work he still had to do. It would only take her a minute to take the garbage to the dumpster. Maverick wouldn't even know.

"I've got it." Becky dragged the heavy bag toward the back door hoping she didn't rip the bag open on a rock as she pulled and tugged it to the dumpster. Thinking of the movies she had watched where the actor always did stupid shit, and she would yell at the television calling them a dumbass, a sudden case of paranoia rushed over her. With a huff, she pushed open the top of the dumpster, then heaved the bag up and over.

Closing the top, she turned to find three men blocking her way to the restaurant. "The entrance is in the front." She gave them a shaky smile and tried to move past them. Seeing fangs and angry glares directed at her, she knew she had made a deadly mistake. *Who was the dumbass now?*

"That her?" the largest one in the middle asked, but his eye stayed on her.

"Yeah, it's her," the other replied.

"Where's my money." The large one stared down at her.

"I don't know what you're talking about." Becky glanced at the back door praying for Maverick to come outside.

"Listen, I don't know or care what James had going with you, but somebody has my money, bitch, and you were the last one seen with him." He took a menacing step toward her. "Now, you are going to take us to his place, now."

Becky was sick to her stomach terrified. She didn't know what to do or say. So she just shook her head, which didn't go over too well. The largest guy grabbed her by the hair fast, pulling her to him. She cried out from the pain.

"This is not a game, bitch." The man's face was so close to hers that spittle shot on her face making her flinch. "I want my fucking money now, and I know, being James's little whore, you know exactly where it is. He liked to brag to his bitches, show off."

She wondered if Maverick would hear her if she screamed loud enough, but the scream seemed to be stuck in her throat.

"Come on, man, before somebody comes looking for her," one of the men said, but Becky didn't know which one since her neck was bent at an odd angle. Before she could react, she was turned and pushed toward a car parked at the entrance to the back employee parking lot. Fear like she had never known almost paralyzed her, but she fought it. She had to think and fast. Her eyes searched for escape, but nothing was coming to her. She knew in her heart if she left in that car, she would never be back. Anger mixed with fear sent a bolt of energy through her body. She couldn't run toward the car, but she could try to take them by surprise and slip past them if the element of surprise was on her side.

Taking a step, she threw herself back while turning. She managed to slip through two of them, her eyes on the back door. "Maverick!" She screamed louder than she had ever screamed in her life. With a sudden wrench back, a large hand had grabbed her shirt. Undeterred, she fought. Becky knew she didn't have a chance against three vampires, but she had to buy some time. She heard her shirt rip and fell forward. Hitting the ground hard, she turned to protect herself, but the men were no longer looking at her.

An inhuman roar sounded behind her and before she could turn to look, Maverick jumped over her, attacking the larger of the three men. She backpedaled out of the way and then screamed when hands gripped her arms.

Earl and Sandra tugged her out of the way. "Oh, my God." Sandra's voice shook.

"Get inside," Earl ordered them, but there was no way Becky was leaving Maverick.

"No, he needs help," Becky said, but as she watched, it became clear that Maverick needed no help at all. Two of the men were already knocked out cold, and Maverick stood over the larger man, his foot on his chest. When he turned to look at her, his eyes were black as midnight, his fangs dipping over his bottom lip.

"Do not fucking leave my sight," he ordered before putting his phone to his ear.

All Becky could do was stare and nod at Maverick, who she realized was a total stranger to her. She didn't know the man who'd taken out three huge vampires in the span of a few minutes.

"Maverick turned into one serious badass," Sandra whispered, putting into words what Becky was having a hard time doing.

Chapter 9

Maverick's rage was to the point if Dusty and Dale didn't arrive soon, he was going to kill the son of a bitch and his thugs. He had Becky sitting where he could see her. A misty rain had started to fall, and she just sat staring at him. He had the old cook, Earl, aiming a gun he had given him at the other two.

"I just want my damn money." The man spat blood but remained sitting against the building where Maverick had thrown him.

Maverick ignored him. It wasn't the time or place. Dusty and Dale would take him back to headquarters and question the asshole. His eyes once again checked on Becky, who looked increasingly lost and afraid, pissing him off. Her safety was his concern, his responsibility.

"You okay, Earl?" Maverick asked, his eyes fixed on Becky.

"Never better," Earl responded, his voice full of excitement. "Can't say stuff like this happens much around this dead town. Kind of exciting."

Maverick chuckled. "If they flinch, shoot." He looked at the two men, who finally come around after being knocked out. They sat perfectly still staring at the gun in Earl's shaking hands.

"Man, I've got nothing against her." The man Maverick stood over nodded toward Becky. "If she'd just tell me where my money is—"

Reaching down, Maverick picked him up by the shirt and slammed him against the wall. "She doesn't know where the fuck your money is. It's in your best interest to never even think about her again, motherfucker." Maverick slammed him against the wall once, then again for good measure. When the man's eyes started to go toward Becky, Maverick growled. "Look at her again and die."

"Holy shit, Mav," Dusty said, walking toward him. "Leave you alone for a couple of days and—"

"Shut up and take the gun from Earl before he kills something," Maverick ordered, his eyes still glaring at the man he held against the wall. Before giving the man over to Dale, he pulled the man's face close to his. "If you ever come near her again, I will hunt you down. Remember my face because it will be your worst nightmare."

Maverick pushed the man toward Dale. "Let me know what you find out from these assholes."

"She okay?" Dale nodded toward Becky.

Maverick nodded but didn't say anything. "I'll come by tomorrow, but let me know what you find out tonight."

"You know I will." Dale walked away with the man while Dusty took the other two, giving them shit all the way to the van. "Good job, man."

Turning, Maverick went straight toward Becky, who sat on a wooden crate. His protective instincts were already in overdrive, but with this woman, they were off the charts. When he had run out the back door and seen her falling helplessly to the ground with Devin DeMarco and his thugs ready to pounce on her, he knew then and there that walking away from her again was something he wasn't going to be able to do.

******

Becky didn't care that it was raining. She wasn't about to move from this spot. Honestly, she didn't think her legs would hold her. Never in her life had she been so scared until she saw Maverick. Then her fear turned to concern for him. She didn't know what she would do if something happened to him in front of her very eyes.

Sandra stumbled out. "I closed the restaurant." She put her arm around Becky as she knelt down. "Are you okay?" With her apron, she cleaned off Becky's chin where it had hit the concrete.

Becky nodded numbly, her voice stuck in her throat.

"He's not the same Maverick we used to know, is he?" Sandra whispered.

"No, he's not," Becky finally responded, a tear slipping down her cheek.

Sandra kissed her cheek. "But what hasn't changed is the love that man has for you." With that, she stood and moved away when Maverick moved toward them.

Becky's gaze locked on his as lightning flashed across the sky behind him. She jumped slightly when thunder boomed. The closer he came, the more she could see the rage in his eyes, the tenseness of his body.

"Becky?" Maverick's voice washed over her and terror slammed into her, making her shake. Tears leaked from her eyes. She stood so fast she stumbled into him, her arms wrapping around him as tightly as they could. The rain came down hard soaking them both. His arms held her just as tightly, and she swore he was shaking also. "I've got you."

He picked her up and walked through the rain to her apartment, then cursed.

"There's a key in the light cover," Becky said into his chest. She felt Maverick reach up while still holding her.

"That won't be happening again." Maverick opened her door, closing it behind them and carefully set her down. He put the key on the counter. "Do not leave a key outside anywhere again. You understand?"

Becky nodded, wrapping her arms around her wet and shaking body. Her eyes roamed over him freely, thinking how sexy he looked wet.

Maverick slowly touched her chin, his frown reaching his eyes. "Are you hurt anywhere else?"

"I don't think so." Becky shook her head. "Are you hurt?"

A small smile replaced his frown. "I'm fine."

"I'm sorry," Becky said and really meant it. "I didn't think—"

"No, you didn't." Maverick cocked an eyebrow.

A loud boom of thunder made her jump. "Are there more people like them looking for me?"

"We don't think so, but we're still working to make sure." Maverick tilted her trembling chin up. "Listen to me. I will not let anyone hurt you."

Becky bobbed her head, her teeth chattering. "I know." She looked deep into his eyes, wanting so much but afraid to take it. Instead, she stood slowly. "Thank you." Not knowing what else to say, she went to turn away to get dried off and changed. Her mind told her to do just that, but her heart begged her to do something else.

With her back to him, her mind and heart warred with each other. Turning her head, she looked at him from over her shoulder and in a split second, she saw him, the Maverick of old staring at her with the desire she would never forget in her lifetime. It was quickly masked with the Maverick she no longer knew.

Unfazed, her heart won the war. She spun and rushed into his arms, pulling his face to her and kissing him with all the anger, want, and love that had filled her for a year. She would have been devastated if he had pushed her away, but his passion matched her own.

Chapter 10

Maverick had to loosen his grip on Becky, afraid he would hurt her. Her kiss was familiar except there was an urgency to it. He was more than happy to meet that urgency with each thrust of his tongue.

He had no idea where this was leading other than him being inside her, and at that moment, he didn't care about anything else. Grabbing her ass, he pulled her up his body and groaned when she wrapped her legs around him tightly.

It had always been like that between them. Hot and passionate, but this was a little different. It was as if they were trying to crawl inside each other. As if they were making up for a lost year. Damn, he had missed her more than he'd even imagined and didn't realize it until that very second.

He worked her shirt off, his mouth exploring a body he remembered well. She responded to him like a starved woman. His hands, along with hers, removed her jeans. He tore her panties, ripping them off her body. Reaching down, he unbuttoned and unzipped his jeans before touching her, making sure she was ready for him. Feeling her wetness, he growled as one finger slipped inside her. She was so fucking tight, and his male pride surged. If she had been with another man since him, it hadn't been recent. The thought of her being with someone else made him want to kill something, but he tapped it down. Using a second finger, he prepped her and then hissed when her hand found his length and began pumping him.

He hated taking her this way. Okay, that was a fucking lie. He loved this urgency but would also love to give her what she deserved, which was a slow love-making session on her bed, but fuck that. He couldn't wait, wouldn't wait.

"Please, Maverick." Her breathless plea hit him hard.

Turning, he pressed her against the wall, fit himself into her and slowly sank her down on his rock-hard cock. "Look at me." When she did, her eyes filled with so much desire, he almost doubled over. He kissed her hard. "I want you to see who is inside you."

"I know who is inside me." Becky's eyes never left his. "The only man who has ever been inside me."

Those words from her lips released something inside Maverick that scared even him. He had to hold himself back. He was stronger now and knew he could break her so easily. He took her mouth again as he pumped inside her, the wall helping keep her stable as he used both hands on her hips to control the motions. He knew she was close, and so was he, but he didn't want this to end. Slowing his pace, he grinned when she groaned in protest and tried to go against him by bucking her hips.

"Damn you, Maverick." Her husky voice breathed against his neck where she had dropped her head against his shoulder. "Please don't make me beg."

Dropping his head, he caught her mouth with his. "Never," he said against her lips and then smiled. "That's for another time."

A tear escaped her eye, sliding down her cheek; he watched its path as he brought her to completion. Her scream of release sent him over the edge while his growl of possessiveness echoed in the room. He held her against him, both of them breathing hard holding on to each other.

"I've missed you so much." Becky's eyes were lowered, but she slowly looked up with uncertainty shadowed in their depths.

Not sure what to say, Maverick dipped his head and kissed her before setting her down. Her body was freezing, goose bumps covering her skin. Tucking himself in and zipping his jeans, Becky stood watching him, fully naked and standing proud as if waiting for something. He knew what that something was, but he wasn't sure if he could promise her anything… yet.

******

When Maverick remained silent after her telling him she had missed him, she turned and walked away. Standing in her bedroom, confusion settled in her chest. She felt lost. What they'd shared, she would do again with or without any promise from him; there were no regrets. But grief threatened to tear her apart. She knew she wasn't losing him again; she never really had him again.

A laugh mixed with a cry escaped her mouth. She was thinking crazy-ass thoughts that made no sense. Maverick Wilder always had that effect on her. With a sigh and a shake of her head, she grabbed dry clothes and dressed. She needed to get back to work. The dinner crowd would be starting soon. If she was to own the restaurant one day, she had to be responsible no matter what life threw at her. This time life threw a cruel curveball called Maverick.

Once done, she reached for the doorknob, but stopped and dropped her hand. How was she going to do this again? Would she survive? This time, she knew by his actions he was going to walk away. What they'd shared was no promise that he would stay, and she would never think that or hold it over his head. No, it was something that had to happen because she wanted it and obviously so had he.

"Shit!" She leaned her head against the door. "Shit. Shit. Shit."

Getting that out and calming her nerves, she opened the door. Maverick was on the phone, but his eyes instantly went to her.

"Yeah, okay," Maverick said into his phone, his eyes shifting away from her. "I'll be there."

Becky sighed, heading toward the refrigerator knowing what was coming. Grabbing a water, she shut the door then turned to face it head on. "Good phone call?"

"Actually very good," Maverick said, then cleared his throat. "They found James's place as well as the books he used, and some of the money."

"Seems he was careless." Becky nodded, taking a drink of water. "So, I'm good now. No one coming after me. It's all clear." Okay, she was rambling.

"It looks like from the books that the only big money owed was to the bastard we caught today." Maverick didn't elaborate. "And they found them on the cameras from the club, so they were there that night, saw you dancing with James and figured you knew his business."

"Awesome," Becky said, a fake grin on her face. "Well, I appreciate—"

"So are we going to stand here and pretend we didn't just fuck in your living room?" Maverick's voice was hard and to the point.

"You were the one who said as soon as I was safe you were gone," Becky shot back. "Your words exactly."

Maverick sighed and rubbed his eyes. "My job is dangerous. I have a lot of enemies."

She may be dying inside, but she'd be damned if she let him know that. "Hey, let me make this easy for you." She grabbed his bag that sat next to the counter and shoved it into his stomach, making him grunt. "Get out." She cocked her eyebrow at him, crossing her arms over her chest.

"What?" Maverick looked at her, shocked.

"If you think I'm going to stand here while you make every

fucking excuse you can think of to walk out of my life, well, you're crazy." She pushed his chest, her voice surprisingly calm. "Get out. I'm throwing you out. Go."

Maverick's eyes narrowed as he dropped his bag. "My job is dangerous. That is not an excuse, but a fact."

"Well, so is mine," Becky shot back. "But I'm not using that as an excuse."

He actually laughed, but it wasn't a funny "ha-ha" laugh. It was an 'I can't believe you just said that' laugh. "You are seriously comparing what you do to what I do?"

"Spoken like a true man." Becky snorted. "You know, Maverick, you just took it upon yourself to walk away from me a year ago. You never asked me if I was willing to take a chance, danger or not."

"I was not willing to take that chance with you, Becky." Maverick growled in irritation.

The words spilled out of her with pained ease. "Then you never really loved me." She pulled no punches because that was exactly what she felt.

He walked up to her so they were nose to nose. "You have no idea what you're talking about." Maverick's breathing was harsh as he turned, punching her wall. With a curse, he picked up his bag and walked out of her door and out of her life, leaving her crushed once again.

Chapter 11

Maverick sat at headquarters finishing up some paperwork. He glanced at his phone. He still had doubts about Becky's safety, so he had hired someone he trusted to sit outside her apartment and keep an eye on her. He knew she was safe because no evidence pointed otherwise, but it was for his peace of mind.

"Hey, was thinking of getting some lunch." Dusty walked in, sitting down in the only empty seat in his small office. "I know a little restaurant with a few sexy waitresses."

"Go away, Dusty," Maverick growled the words, not in the mood.

"Dude, come on." Dusty sighed. "What in the hell is wrong with you to let a woman like her go? She is fucking hot and obviously into you. Hell, if you're done, then care if I give it a shot?"

Maverick was over his desk before Dusty could move. He was on top of Dusty ready to plow his fist into his face until he saw him smiling like an idiot. "I'm about ready to beat your face in. Why the fuck are you smiling?"

"Because you're in lurve, my friend, and too fucking stupid to do anything about it." Dusty sat up when Maverick pushed off him with a curse.

"She doesn't deserve to live this kind of life." Maverick leaned against his desk, then reached out a hand to Dusty, pulling him up.

"Yeah, well, bullshit on that." Dusty brushed himself off. "It seems Barry, Mike, and Don would disagree with you on that since all of them have families. I think you're a pussy, to be honest with you."

"Do you want your ass kicked?" Maverick growled without much heat behind the threat.

"Did you even ask her what kind of life she wanted?" Dusty asked, his eyebrow cocked. Seeing his face, Dusty nodded. "Of course you didn't. Seriously, bro. Give her a choice. If she doesn't want to take a chance, then she isn't even worth your time, but I saw her in action, and she's a badass who can take care of herself pretty much. But you better get your ass in gear before someone else steps in, just sayin'."

"What the fuck does that mean?" Maverick straightened, looking down at Dusty. He looked as if he didn't want to say anything, but Maverick knew better. Dusty was always running his damn mouth about something.

"Casey, the Enforcer you hired to watch her, told me he's been talking to her. He thinks she's hot," Dusty said, then grimaced. "Damn, dude. I'm sorry. I guess you need to know exactly who you hire to do some of your jobs."

"That motherfucker." Maverick roared as he stomped his way out of his office.

What Maverick didn't see was Dusty chuckling and shaking his head. "Damn, wouldn't want to be Casey."

******

Becky had just finished work. She knew the guy sitting outside her apartment had been hired by Maverick to keep an eye on her, which both pissed her off yet made her feel a little safer. Her eyes went to the hole in her wall. She tried to ignore it, but it was right there. She needed to get it fixed, tell Casey she was fine, and wipe every memory of Maverick from her life.

Before she could even put her bag down, she heard squealing tires and then men yelling at each other. One voice was very familiar. Running to her door, she threw it open. Maverick was pulling Casey out of his car through the window.

"Maverick!" she screamed, running toward them. Casey was young, and she could tell he was no match for Maverick. "Stop! What in the hell is wrong with you?"

"Go back inside." Maverick ordered, but she wasn't listening.

"What the fuck?" Casey tried to pry himself away from Maverick.

"I hired you to do a fucking job." Maverick was in his face.

"And I'm doing that job." Casey looked confused and a little scared, but who wouldn't? Maverick was a frightening sight when he was pissed off.

"She is not available," Maverick yelled, pointing toward Becky.

Both Becky and Casey looked at each other. "Ah, okay," Casey said, staring at Maverick. "What in the hell does that have to do with my job?"

Cocking his head, Maverick dropped Casey with a curse. "Fucking Dusty."

Casey's mouth snapped open, and then he looked pissed. "Dusty told you that I was trying to pick her up?" His face turned red with rage. "I swear to God, I'm going to kill him this time. What the fuck!"

"Yeah, you better get to him before me," Maverick said, his tone less harsh. He reached out, straightening Casey's shirt. "Sorry, man."

"Dude, you know I would never—"

"Yeah, I know. Go ahead and take off." Maverick nodded toward his car.

Becky watched what was happening, shocked to see Maverick looking a little embarrassed. Once Casey was gone, she put her hand on her hip.

"You thought Casey and I were...?" She cocked her eyebrow at him.

"No," Maverick said, shaking his head. "Dusty.... You know what, never mind. It's not important."

"There it is." Becky gave a bitter laugh. "When it has to do with me, it's never important." She turned and walked into the apartment.

She screamed when the door slammed behind her. Turning, her eyes landed on Maverick, who towered over her. "How in the fuck can you say that? You are the only thing that is important," Maverick shouted. Shaking his head, his voice lowered. "Becky, knowing what I am, what I do and the danger, what choice would you have made a year ago?"

With her heart beating wildly in her chest, Becky eyed him with surprise. Vulnerability filled his eyes. "The same choice I would make today, Maverick," she said, her voice strong and true. "You. My choice would have been and is you."

When Maverick reached out and pulled her to him, she was sure her heart would explode. "I'm sorry," he whispered in her hair. Instinctively, she closed her eyes, soaking in his words, breathing in the moment. "I never meant to hurt you. I just wanted to keep you safe."

"I love you, Maverick Wilder, and you are the same person to me, fangs and all." She looked up at him, cupping his cheek. "I never stopped loving you."

A small squeak escaped her lips when Maverick picked her up and headed to her bedroom. "I love you, Becky." He nudged her door open then slammed it shut with his boot. "And I owe you slow lovemaking, so I hope you're well rested."

The grin on his face and the heat in his voice was almost more than she could take. "If I remember correctly, I was never well rested where you were concerned." Becky smiled up at him, never happier than she was at that very moment. "And I wouldn't want it any other way."

******

Dusty stood next to Maverick, spotting Casey in the crowd. "You know, you never did thank me." Dusty reached up, tugging at his tie.

"For what?" Maverick frowned, but his eyes stayed glued to the back of the church.

"Ah, for this." Dusty threw his hand out in a grand gesture. "If not for me, we wouldn't be standing here. Unfortunately, Casey almost died in the process, but I made this happen."

"Shut the fuck up, Dusty." Maverick rolled his eyes.

"Dude, some respect. We are in church." Dusty grinned, his eyes watching Becky's best friend walk up the aisle. "So, does Sandra have a boyfriend I may need to kill 'cause she is fuc... freaking hot!"

Maverick looked around Dusty to Dale, who looked uncomfortable and out of place standing in his black tux. His gaze returned to Dusty. "You know, I think I owe you one."

"Damn straight you do." Dusty smirked then winked at Sandra.

"Hey, Dale," Maverick whispered toward Dale. "You remember your ex, Betty?"

Dale gave him a confused look before nodding.

"Dusty here went out with her after you broke if off." Maverick grinned when Dusty grimaced and squeezed his eyes closed when Dale growled low in his throat. Maverick leaned close to Dusty. "Now we're even."

Maverick laughed, but it caught in his throat as he stared at the most beautiful woman at the back of the church. With Earl at her side, Becky took his breath away. Her white strapless dress was plain but absolutely gorgeous, hugging every curve on her body. Her hair hung loose down her back the way he liked it. He fell in love with her all over again at that very moment.

"Holy shit." Dusty whistled low.

"I will kill you, church or not," Maverick warned with a smile before stepping down to meet Becky, who beamed at him. Earl placed her hand in his then kissed her on the cheek before taking a seat.

"I'm an idiot," Maverick murmured, reaching up and cupping her cheek.

"What?" Becky leaned into his touch with a frown.

"I could have done this a year ago." He bent down and kissed her softly. "I love you, Becky soon-to-be Wilder. You're mine, and I'm never letting go."

CPSIA information can be obtained
at www.ICGtesting.com
Printed in the USA
LVOW07s1027150517
534572LV00015B/471/P